TINY
PENGUINS
and the New Baby

JANE PORTER

For Alf, Clem and Gertie, with love
J.P.

SIMON & SCHUSTER
First published in Great Britain in 2021 by Simon & Schuster UK Ltd
1st Floor, 222 Gray's Inn Road, London, WC1X 8HB
Text and illustrations copyright © 2021 Jane Porter • The right of Jane Porter
to be identified as the author and illustrator of this work has been asserted by her in
accordance with the Copyright, Designs and Patents Act, 1988 • All rights reserved,
including the right of reproduction in whole or in part in any form • A CIP catalogue
record for this book is available from the British Library upon request.
978-1-4711-7341-7 (PB) • 978-1-4711-7342-4 (eB)
Printed in China • 10 9 8 7 6 5 4 3 2 1

TINY
PENGUINS
and the New Baby

JANE PORTER

SIMON & SCHUSTER

London   New York   Sydney   Toronto   New Delhi

Have you ever wondered who sorts out
the squeaks and the leaks in every home?

It's us!

We're the Tiny Penguins . . .

There's Hetty
and Betty the
Toolbox Twins,

Paintbrush Pete,

Little tiny Teeny,

and me,
Handy Candy.

We love helping humans, but our number one rule is:
Stay out of sight – our work is TOP SECRET!

Here we are, helping little Gertie at Number 5 –
we're going to make her shoes shine like diamonds
with our special polish.

But hold on – what has Teeny spotted under the bed?

Oh dear. It's Gertie, looking *very* sad. But why?

We'd better take a look around . . .

Ah. Now we understand.
All Gertie's people are busy –
busy looking at a tiny new human.

When Tiny Penguins hatch, they have to be fed
and looked after all day long – and it's the same
for humans. There's no time left to play.

Gertie's grown-ups are going to be busy for quite a while and we don't want Gertie to be lonely.

It's time to break our number one rule . . .

and say . . .

Hello, Gertie!

I don't think she's ever seen anyone quite like us before!

Look at that smile — we're **definitely** going to be friends.

Let's start by teaching her our special penguin waddle.

Oh, she's very good at this! Well . . . good for a human!

In fact, Gertie's good at all
sorts of things –

especially driving . . .

and building houses!

We do **all** the important jobs with Gertie – things like making pictures . . .

and cookies.

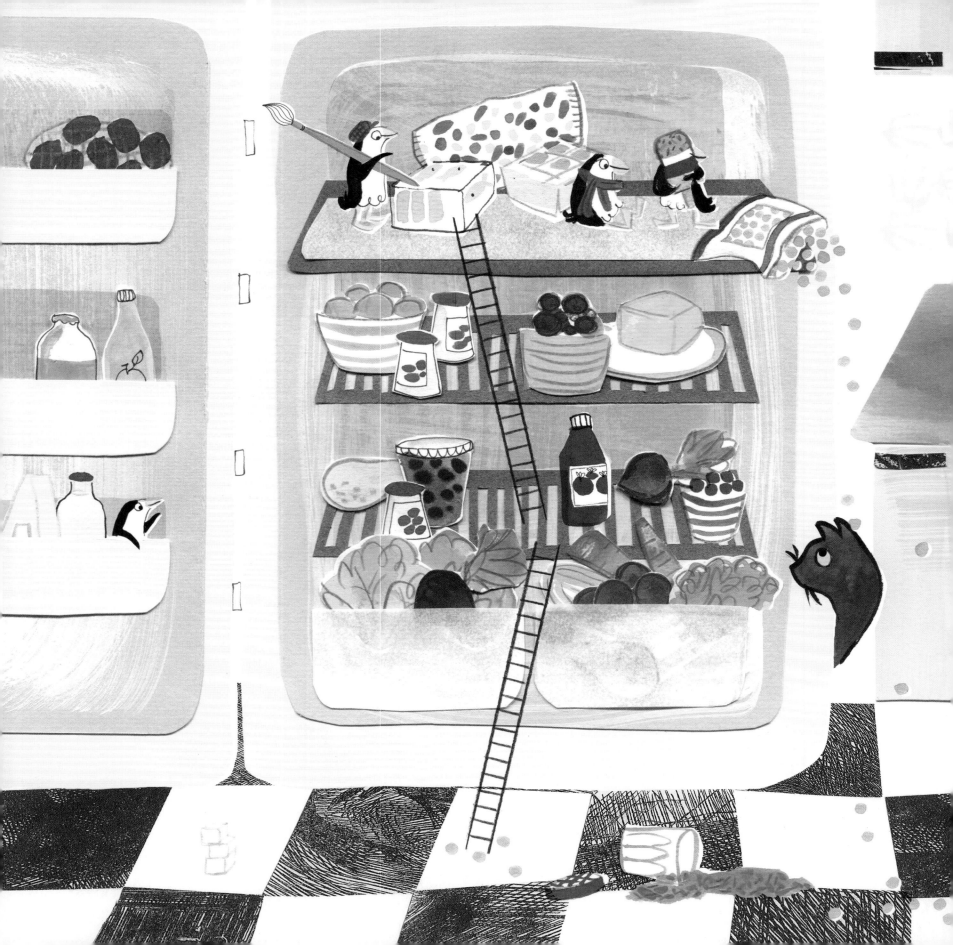

Getting things sorted in the ice cave is a useful job when it's hot. Gertie loves the stripy icebergs the humans keep in there.

All that hard work can make us a bit sticky
so every evening we all go for a swim.

We love to make a penguin pyramid!
Up you go, Hetty and Betty!
Nice work, Pete!

And now, Teeny,
on the top –

1, 2, 3...

Oh no! The baby's seen us!

Watch out . . .
oooops!

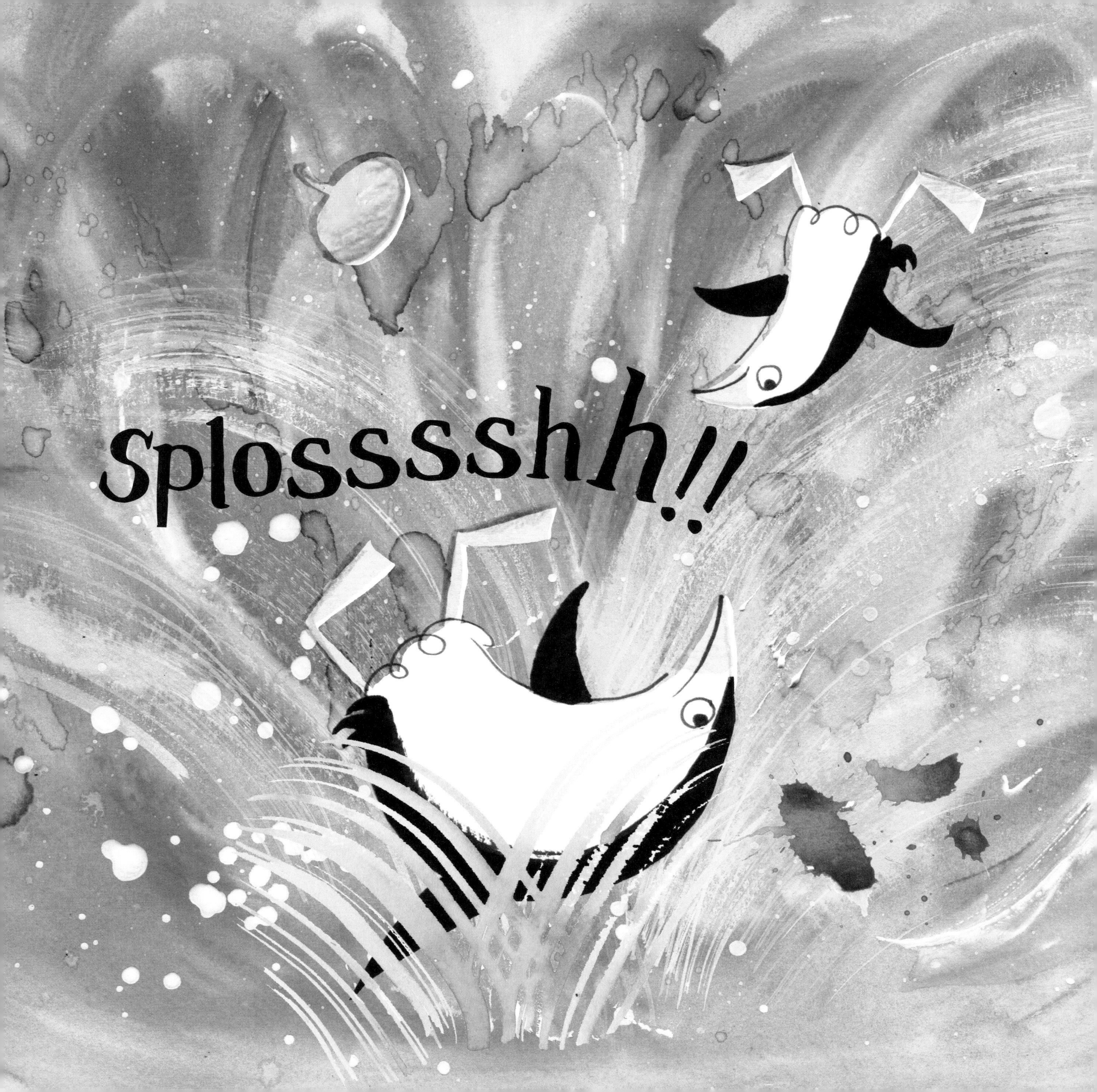
Splossshh!!

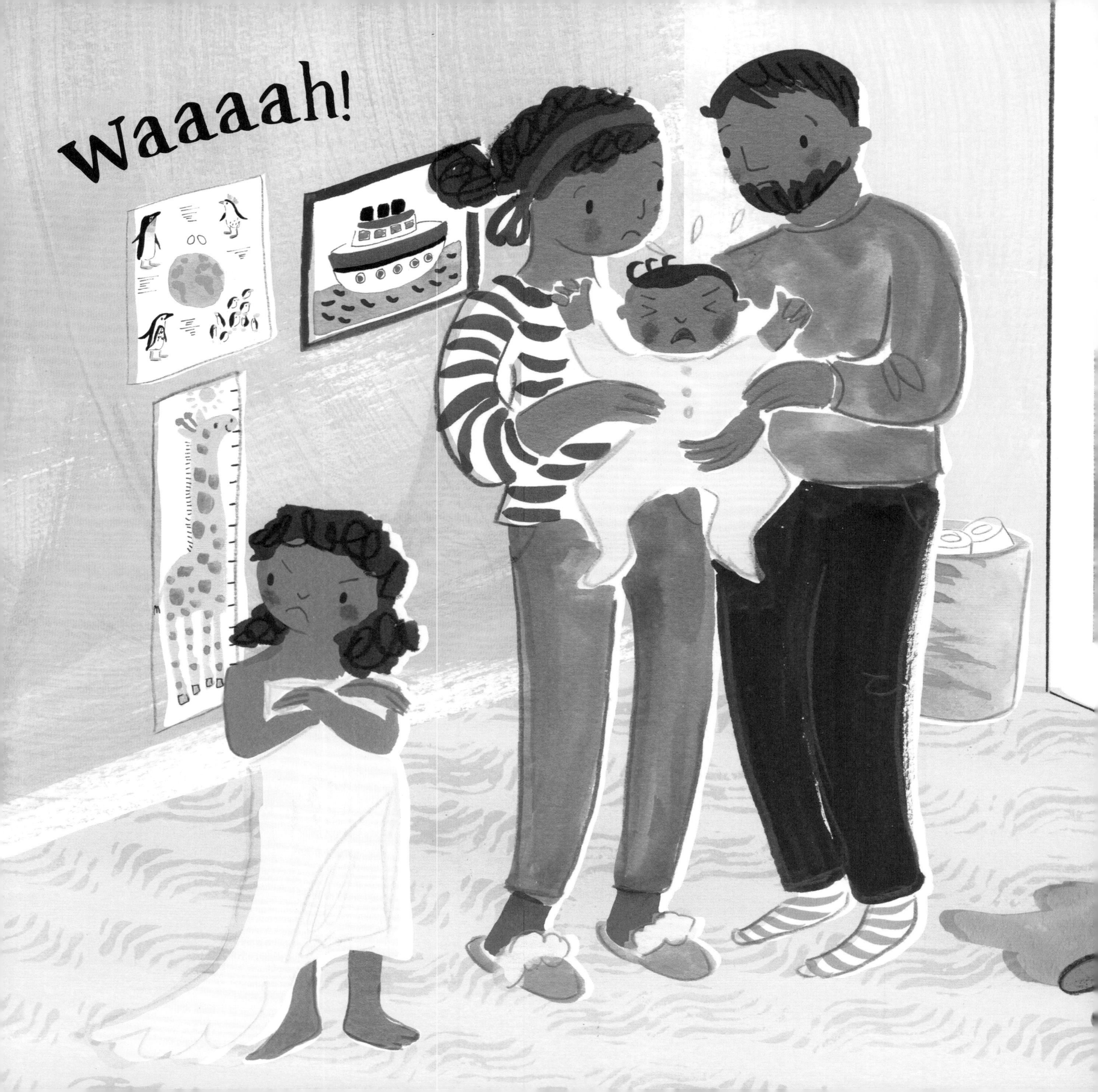
Waaaaah!

Oh dear, the tiny human doesn't seem to like getting wet. How strange! He's making a loud noise and he won't stop – but worse than that, we've got Gertie into trouble.

We need to fix this – but how? Let's have a big think.

Should we oil him?

Pete thinks we
should paint him . . .

and Hetty suggests
using the special polish!

Teeny's doing his thinking waddle,

and watching him has given Gertie a brilliant idea!

The tiny human has never seen
waddling like THIS before.
He's stopped the noise!

Listen –
that's a MUCH nicer sound.

It turns out that Gertie
and the baby love waddling . . .

and cuddling . . .

and snuggling
together.

Gertie's not sad any more.
Our work here is done.

Did you say YOU have
some squeaks and leaks?

Or even a brand new baby?

Maybe we'll come to YOUR home next . . .

See you soon!